Be My Friend

joan walsh anglund

Little Simon

With loving wishes for
Aurora,
Jane,
Teddy,
and Amelia

LITTLE SIMON
An imprint of Simon & Schuster Children's Publishing Division
1230 Avenue of the Americas, New York, New York 10020
Copyright © 2000 by Joan Walsh Anglund
All rights reserved including the right of reproduction in whole or in part in any form.
LITTLE SIMON and colophon are registered trademarks of Simon & Schuster.
Manufactured in China
First Edition   10 9 8 7 6 5 4 3 2 1
ISBN 0-689-82638-9

This book belongs to

....

Come, be my friend,
and together we'll play.

We'll be happy and busy
all through the day.

Together we can swing from a tree,

we can crawl through the grass.

We can lie on a hill
and watch the clouds pass.

We can throw a big ball,
we can hit with a bat.

We can start our own zoo
with my dog and your cat.

We can fish . . .

if we wish,

we can fly . . . if we try.

We can dance, we can swim,
we can eat cherry pie.

We can play on a train.

We can splash in the rain.

We can row on a lake.

We can cook, we can bake.

We can ride on our bikes.

We can run like the wind.

We can laugh, we can play . . .

Come, be my friend!